W9-AQV-749

Christmas at the Top of the World

WRITTEN & ILLUSTRATED BY

Tim Coffey

SCHOLASTIC INC.

New York   Toronto   London   Auckland   Sydney
Mexico City   New Delhi   Hong Kong   Buenos Aires

No part of this publication may be reproduced, stored in a retrieval system,
or transmitted in any form or by any means, electronic, mechanical, photocopying,
recording, or otherwise, without written permission of the publisher.
For information regarding permission, write to Albert Whitman & Company,
6340 Oakton Street, Morton Grove, IL 60053-2723.

ISBN 0-439-72755-3

Text and Illustrations copyright © 2003 by Tim Coffey. All rights reserved.
Published by Scholastic Inc., 557 Broadway, New York, NY 10012, by arrangement with
Albert Whitman & Company. SCHOLASTIC and associated logos are trademarks
and/or registered trademarks of Scholastic Inc.

12 11 10 9 8 7 6 5 4 3 2 1   5 6 7 8 9/0

Printed in the U.S.A.   40

First Scholastic printing, November 2004

The paintings were rendered in acrylic on watercolor paper textured with gesso.
The design is by Carol Gildar.

In memory of Dan

Little Reindeer loved winter. That was because Papa would tell him his favorite story at sleep time.

"When I was your age, I discovered a place where the ground rises up to the sky and you are high enough to touch the stars," Papa said. "A magical place, at the top of the world."

Where could this be? Little Reindeer wondered. He would wonder every night until he fell asleep.

One frosty night, Papa told Mama and Little Reindeer he was going on a journey.

"I'm leaving tomorrow," he said gently, "but I'll be back on Christmas."

Little Reindeer's ears perked up. "I want to go, too!" he said.

"One day you'll go," said Papa. "Just wait."

In the morning, Little Reindeer and Mama kissed Papa goodbye and watched him disappear deep into the woods. Little Reindeer had lots of questions.

"Where did Papa go?" he asked Mama. "How long until he's back? How long until Christmas?"

"He's up north, at the top of the world," Mama replied. "And when the north wind feels warm and smells sweet, it'll be Christmas Eve. You'll know," she added. "All the animals will know."

It was hard to wait for Papa. At night, while Mama slept, Little
Reindeer stared at the sky. He remembered Papa's story about a
magical place. *A place where you are high enough to touch the stars.*
Days and days passed, and then—one night felt different.

The air smelled warm and sweet. It was the wind from the north. "The top of the world," he whispered. That was where Papa was, right now.

It was Christmas Eve. Little Reindeer couldn't wait anymore. He was going to find Papa!

The other animals saw him go.

Little Reindeer walked for a long time.
At last he turned to look back. Every creature of the
North Woods was behind him. And Mama, too!

He remembered what she'd said about Christmas Eve:
All the animals will know. Now they were following Little Reindeer
to the top of the world.

At the top of a hill, Little Reindeer stopped, and
the other animals stopped, too.

They heard only silence, and then they saw the
place where the earth touched the heavens.

There were green stars, red stars,
blue stars, too—yellow and white
twinkling stars—they were close
enough to touch, just as Papa had said.
Little Reindeer made his way
toward the biggest, brightest star.

In the center of the village, the star glittered and shone at the top of a beautiful tree. It was like no other star Little Reindeer had ever seen.

"But where is Papa?" he wondered.

He could hear bells jingling up in the sky. Something was coming—he could hear it louder and closer. Something big! In a flash, it swooped down to the ground.

What was it? The other animals gathered around, and Little Reindeer nudged his way to the front of the crowd.

An old man came
over to Little Reindeer,
knelt down, and patted
his head softly.

"I know who you are,"
the man said with a twinkle
in his eye. "You must be
here to see your papa."

And that's when Little Reindeer saw Papa by the sleigh. Papa was leading all the other reindeer!

"This is the magic place, isn't it?" whispered Little Reindeer. "I couldn't wait."

"You waited as long as you could," said Papa. "It's Christmas Eve."

It was time for the
kind old man, Papa, and the
other reindeer to bring the
peace and magic of this place
to the rest of the world.

Little Reindeer stood
with Mama and watched
Papa soar above the village
into the snowy night.

Then he snuggled against Mama and fell asleep.
It would be Christmas soon, and Little Reindeer was
on top of the world.